Fun Poems For Kids!!

Poetry by Chris Husband

ISBN: 9798867789053

DEDICATION

To everyone that loves to smile!

Contents

Breakfast Hero…………………….3

What do you feed a ghost?.....4

House Spider…………………….5

The Brownie's Poem……………6

Granny's Nightie……………….8

Lobster, crab………………………10

Chippy Tea……………………11

Frog in my throat……………….13

1, 2, 3, Banana……………………15

Good Morning Mr. Magpie…..16

My Magical Bearded Friend….18

The Goal…………………………20

One Lost Glove……………….21

Charlie's Dreams……………….22

Granny's for Tea…………………24

A Quality Street Christmas…..26

About The Author………………28

ACKNOWLEDGMENTS

In putting this small collection together, I would like to thank all of the people who provided the inspiration for me to put mouse to screen.

To Charlie the Cat, who shared his innermost secrets and dreams with me.

To all the Grannies out there – watch the windy weather when your washing is on the line!

.

Breakfast Hero

You surely are everything
I could want you to be.
The spread on my toast,
The milk in my tea.
The crunch in my cereal,
The oats in my bowl.
The tang in my juice,
The jam on my roll.
The crisp of my bacon,
The beans on my plate.
The sausage so juicy,
The black pudding I ate.
The 'wake me up' coffee,
The greasy fried bread.
The smell of your cooking,
Gets me out of my bed.
You surely are everything.
I could want you to be,
Oh beautiful breakfast.
A hero to me!

What do you feed a ghost?

When you invite a spirit over
To your house for tea,
Have you got the first idea
Of what that meal should be?
Will they be able to stomach
Lots of Jam and Bread?
Do you give a cream cake to
A person who might be dead?
Have they got the taste buds
For mugs of steaming tea?
Would they love the treat
That is Cherries Jubilee?
One thing is for certain,
You can always feed a ghost,
With anything that is usually served
On hot buttered toast.

House Spider

She sneaks around
Both day and night,
Her only aim
To give a fright,
To all the people
In her home,
And anywhere else
She wants to roam.

You cannot hear her,
Or see her approach.
She is half the size
Of a cockroach.
She can walk up walls,
And ceilings so high.
Her very sight can
Make grown men cry.

They try to catch her
With a glass or jug,
But she quickly dives
Underneath the rug.
If they manage to catch her,
And show her the door.
She is soon right back in
Scuttling fast across the floor.

The Brownie's Poem

Once I was a Rainbow,
Red, Orange, Green and Blue;
Yellow, Indigo and Violet,
Then up to the Brownies I flew.

I made my Brownie promise
To serve both King and community.
To always do my best for
Others, and for me.

I shall try to be true to myself,
Thinking of others is the Brownie way.
I will develop my own beliefs,
Doing a good deed every day.

To be a Brownie is an honour
But also so much fun.
With the help of our Brown Owl,
We always get things done.

Dressed smartly in brown and gold
Of the Sixes I am so proud.

And every time I wear the uniform
I shall declare out loud:

**"I promise that I will do my best, to be true to
myself and develop my beliefs, to serve the King
and my community, to help other people and to
keep the Brownie law."**

Granny's Nightie

Granny washed her nightie,
And hung it on the line.
She thought that it would dry outside,
As the weather was so fine.

Just as she had pegged it out,
A great big cloud appeared.
The wind began to blow and blow,
and just as Granny feared;

It blew away her nightie.
It blew it left and righty.
Up and up and up it soared,
Like a lovely, flowery kitey.

Grandad got an awful frighty,
When he suddenly caught sighty,
From his greenhouse in the garden,
Of Granny's airborne nightie.

It carried on its flighty
Right across the building sitey
The crane driver looked confused when
Past his eyes flew Granny's nightie.

With a pattern pink and whitey,
Over treetops tall and mighty,
Now just a dot in the distance,
Farewell to Granny's nightie.

Lobster, crab

Lobster, crab,
bubble, bubble, bubble
Lobster, crab,
always finding trouble
Lobster, crab,
Swim, swim, swim,
Lobster, crab,
In the sea they skim
Lobster, crab,
Push, push, push,
Lobster, crab,
Always in a rush
Lobster, crab,
Snore, snore, snore
Lobster, crab,
Sleeping on the shore
Lobster, crab,
Always nice and neat
Lobster, crab,
With wellies on their feet

Chippy Tea

Just finished work this evening
Now what to eat, let's see
Only one more day till weekend so
It must be Chippy Tea!

Chippy Tea
Chippy Tea
That's what it must be!
Chippy Tea
Chippy Tea
That's the one for me!

Now what grub do I fancy?
Fish, chips and mushy peas?
Steak pudding with lots of gravy?
Beef burger with lots of cheese?

Chippy Tea
Chippy Tea
That's what it must be!
Chippy Tea
Chippy Tea
That's the one for me!

Jumbo sausage, such a favourite
Curry sauce and lots of scraps
Meat pies that burn your lips off
Steak and kidney pie perhaps?

Chippy Tea
Chippy Tea
That's what it must be!
Chippy Tea
Chippy Tea
That's the one for me!

I might plump for fried chicken,
But that tends to be dry
That's it! A massive pile of chips
Topped with meat 'n tata pie!

Chippy Tea
Chippy Tea
That's what it must be!
Chippy Tea
Chippy Tea
That's the one for me!

(This is now a fabulous song by Susan Osborne
https://www.facebook.com/SusansLancashireLaffs)

Frog in my throat

Tony Toad had a terrible cold,
So bad it made him weep.
He caught it when he went to swim
And dived down way too deep.
It made him cough
And cough
And cough
So much he couldn't sleep.

Tony made a cup of tea,
Blew it, then tried a sip.
But when he took a great big swig
He nearly burned his lip.
Which made him cough
And cough
And cough
And almost made him slip.

He went to see the doctor.
Who took his temperature
The doctor said "That's very strange!
You're much too hot, I'm sure."
And Tony coughed
And coughed
And coughed
But didn't get a cure.

Tony had a visitor,
His good friend Colin Stoat.
He looked at Tony, then he said
"Ah! I've had a thought."
He shook Tony's back,
Then gave it a whack
And said, "You've a frog in your throat!"

After one giant cough,
Then a very loud 'pop!'
A small and puzzled frog
Leaped down with a hop.
They laughed
And laughed
And laughed
So much they couldn't stop

1, 2, 3, Banana

One banana
Two banana
Three banana
One more makes it Four

One step
Two step
Three step
On the floor

One slip
Two slip
Three slip
Crash into the door

One crack
Two crack
Three crack
Ow! My head is sore

Good Morning Mr. Magpie

Good Morning Mr. Magpie
Was my greeting to this bird.

Good Morning Mr. Magpie
But I don't think that he heard.

Good Morning Mr. Magpie
I gave another try.

Good Morning Mr. Magpie
But he just hopped on by.

The very next day I thought
That I would try to catch his eye.

Good Morning Mr. Magpie I said
But he just left me high and dry.

So I spoke to him quite brusquely
"It's common courtesy you lack!"

And with that single outburst
He jumped upon my back.

He rode me round the garden
He rode me up the street.

He leaped down to the pavement
And pecked upon my feet.

He jumped up on my shoulder
And pulled away my cap.

His beak nibbled my earlobe
And his feathers gave a slap.

I begged for him to leave me
To stop without delay.

Then all at once he spread his wings
And grandly flew away.

So since this painful episode
I remember just to try

To say this simple greeting
Good Morning Mr. Magpie!

This poem can also be bought as a Picture Book.
Check out www.chrishusband.com

My Magical Bearded Friend

My friend has a fine crop of whiskers,
That completely envelope his chin.
They make him look just like a badger,
With a pleasantly welcoming grin.

I think that he must oil them daily,
Each strand is precisely controlled.
Like whispers of finely spun silver,
Their lustre a sight to behold.

Such magnificent facial hair makes him
So distinguished and regal to see.
An important old Gent about town,
Who surely has places to be.

He carries a cane of pure walnut,
And his hat is as tall as a tree.
Edged with the richest of satin,
And a brooch made from gold filigree.

His suit is from Saville Row tailors,
No smarter I'm sure could be found.
His boots are the softest of leather,
Whose steps barely raise up a sound.

The scent of cologne is exquisite
And leaves passers-by in a trance.

A tie pin of opals and diamonds
Just adds to his air of romance.

So if your paths cross accidentally,
And you happen to capture his gaze,
Touch the peak of your cap and bow grandly
And utter this respectful phrase.

"Good Day Sir, I trust you are well, Sir?"
Then listen as he passes by
With his quiet, melodious timbre
You may just then catch his reply.

"A Good Day to you too dearest friend"
"Fine weather we're having today"
Then with a theatrical wave of his hand
He will silently hurry away.

If you turn for just one more look
At his marvellous, lustrous beard
You may find that my friend is no longer in sight.
He has magically disappeared!

This poem can also be bought as a Picture Book.
Check out www.chrishusband.com

The Goal

"Gimme the ball! Gimme the ball!"
The centre forward gives the call.
"On me 'ead son! On me 'ead!"
Shouts the man with feet of lead.
Down the flank the winger flies.
"'Ere you go, try this for size!"
The ball curls up across the box,
The striker jumps out of his socks.
Here it comes now, fast approaching.
This sharpshooter needs no coaching.
The ball arrives, right on his bonce.
From the corner of his eye he spies at once.
The centre half is six feet six
And built just like a ton of bricks!
Get the ball or get the man.
He's going to get whatever he can.
The whistle blows, but where's the ball?
Everyone cheers. Yes, it's a goal!
But does the striker know the score?
No, he's flat out on the floor!

One Lost Glove

Oh lost glove! Oh lost Glove!
Forlornly laying there.
Never again to know the joy
of living as a pair.
Your partner now is destined
to a life of lone despair.
Your owner now one cold hand,
unless they have a spare?
Oh lost glove! Oh lost Glove!
Forlornly laying there.

Charlie's Dreams

Charlie loved to sleep all day,
All warm and cosy in his bed.
With a great big smile, he'd dream away,
Waking briefly to be fed.

Oh what adventures he would find
Whilst tucked up in his cot!
The birds that he would sneak behind.
Mouse captures he would plot.

Charlie liked to have great fun
With Ted the dog next door.
Along the neighbour's wall he'd run
So Ted would bark some more.

He'd stroll inside the grocer's shop
Getting under people's feet.
Then jump up on the counter top
And steal a tasty treat.

Hiding from the milkman
He'd jump out and make him scream.
Milk bottles would fall out from the van
And Charlie would lick the cream.

Charlie would find the warmest spot
Upon his human's knee.
But when he was getting far too hot
He would shade under a tree.

The thing that Charlie likes the most
As any cat's human knows,
Is to be tucked up, warm as toast
In a lovely, dreamy doze.

Granny's for Tea

On a Sunday we go round to Granny's
For tea and cake and treats.
Pies galore
And lots, lots more
Plus bags and bags of sweets

The thing we like most of all
Is to taste her homemade tarts.
But while we all scoff
One thing puts us off
Grandad's dreadful farts!

It really is quite disturbing
While Granny toasts the crumpets,
For Grandad's eructation
To cause such consternation
And sound like a fanfare of trumpets.

While we sit down to eat an iced bun
Or some other delicious cream cake
It's Grandad's loud toots
That reverb through our boots
And make the room properly shake.

Grandma just laughs at his antics
"Oh Jim you're a terrible tease.
It's the things that you munch

Like those baked beans for lunch
Or that extra pile of mushy peas".

It's best to sit close to the window
That is open as wide as can be
For the stench from his chair
Has us gasping for air
It's like dozens of over-ripe brie.

When the time comes to head home to our place
There is just time before we depart
For our Grandad with style
And a mischievous smile
To push out one more ginormous fart!

A Quality Street Christmas

Christmas is coming
And grandad's getting fat.
Someone put the Quality Street
Right where grandad's sat.

He's groaning, full of turkey
As he waits for the King's speech,
But those pesky little sweeties
Are just within his reach.

He knows he shouldn't really
But they're so hard to ignore,
And every time he's had enough
His brain thinks "just one more".

In his shame he's started to hide
The wrappers in his chair.
His seat is rustling when he moves
As the dog gives him a stare.

With molars full of toffee,
And nuts stuck in his gum,
He needs to rinse his dentures,
But there's evidence 'neath his bum.

Then he has a brainwave
To put the wrappers back in the tin.

He rolls them to a great big ball
And furtively drops them in.

Now, as he stands up proudly
To deliberately replace the lid.
The dog gives him a knowing look
Saying "who are you trying to kid?"

Grandad winks back at him
As he moves towards the door.
He gently lifts the lid back off.
"Go on then, just one more!"

About The Author

Chris Husband – Poet and all-round good egg!

I love to write poems for both kids and adults. It brings me great joy and I hope it does for you too.

I urge you all to have a go at writing some poems yourself and if you want to get in touch to show me some of your work, please do not hesitate to do so through my website – www.chrishusband.com

I look forward to reading your work and I hope you enjoy this book!

Fun Poems for Kids

Printed in Great Britain
by Amazon

45908742R00020